The Adventures of
Paddy the Beaver

Bedtime Story-Books
By THORNTON W. BURGESS

The Bedtime Story-Books

The Adventures of Paddy the Beaver

By THORNTON W. BURGESS

Illustrated by HARRISON CADY

PUBLISHERS

Grosset & Dunlap

NEW YORK

BY ARRANGEMENT WITH LITTLE, BROWN & COMPANY
PRINTED IN THE UNITED STATES OF AMERICA

The Adventures of Paddy the Beaver

Contents

[*v*]

CONTENTS

Illustrations

ILLUSTRATIONS

I

Paddy the Beaver
Begins Work

Work, work all the night
While the stars are shining bright;
Work, work all the day;
I have got no time to play.

THIS little rhyme Paddy the
Beaver made up as he toiled
at building the dam which was to
make the pond he so much desired
deep in the Green Forest. Of course
it wasn't quite true, that about

working all night and all day. Nobody could do that, you know, and keep it up. Everybody has to rest and sleep. Yes, and everybody has to play a little to be at their best. So it wasn't quite true that Paddy worked all day after working all night. But it was true that Paddy had no time to play. He had too much to do. He had had his playtime during the long summer, and now he had to get ready for the long, cold winter.

Now, of all the little workers in the Green Forest, on the Green Meadows, and in the Smiling Pool, none can compare with Paddy the Beaver, not even his cousin, Jerry Muskrat. Happy Jack Squirrel and Striped Chipmunk store up food for the long, cold months when rough Brother North Wind and Jack Frost rule, and Jerry Muskrat builds a fine house wherein to keep warm and comfortable, but all this is as nothing to the work of Paddy the Beaver.

As I said before, Paddy had had a long playtime through the summer. He had wandered up and down the Laughing Brook. He had followed it way up to the place where it started. And all the time he had been studying and studying to make sure that he wanted to stay in the Green Forest. In the first place, he had to be sure that there was plenty of the kind of food that he likes. Then he had to be equally sure that he could make a pond near where this particular food grew. Last of all, he had to satisfy himself that if he did make a pond and build a home, he would be reasonably safe in it. And all these things he had done in his playtime. Now he was ready to go to work, and when Paddy begins work, he sticks to it until it is finished. He says that is the only way to succeed, and you know and I know that he is right.

Now Paddy the Beaver can see at night just as Reddy Fox and Peter Rabbit and Bobby Coon can, and he likes the night best, because he feels safest then. But he can see in the daytime too, and when he feels that he is perfectly safe and no one is watching, he works then too. Of course, the first thing to do was to build a dam across the Laughing Brook to make the pond he so much needed. He chose a low, open place deep in the Green Forest, around the edge of which grew many young aspen trees, the bark of which is his favorite food. Through the middle of this open place flowed the Laughing Brook.

At the lower edge was just the place for a dam. It would not have to be very long, and when it was finished and the water was stopped in the Laughing Brook, it would just have to flow over the low, open place and make a pond there. Paddy's eyes twinkled when he first saw it. It was right then that he made up his mind to stay in the Green Forest.

So now that he was ready to begin his dam he went up the Laughing Brook to a place where alders and willows grew, and there he began work; that work was the cutting of a great number of trees by means of his big front teeth which were given him for just this purpose. And as he worked, Paddy was happy, for one can never be truly happy who does no work.

Paddy Plans a Pond

PADDY THE BEAVER was busy cutting down trees for the dam he had planned to build. Up in the woods of the North from which he had come to the Green Forest, he had learned all about tree-cutting and dam-building and canal-digging and house-building. Paddy's father and mother had been very wise in the Beaver world, and Paddy had been quick to learn. So now he knew just what to do and the best way of doing it. You know, a great many people waste time and labor doing things the wrong way, so that they have to be done over again. They forget to be sure they are right, and so they go ahead until they find they are wrong, and all their work goes for nothing.

But Paddy the Beaver isn't this kind. Paddy would never have leaped into the spring with the steep sides without looking, as 'Grandfather Frog did. So now he carefully picked out the trees to cut. He could not afford to waste time cutting down a tree that wasn't going to be just what he wanted when it was down. When he was sure that the tree was right, he looked up at the top to find out whether, when he had cut it, it would fall clear of other trees. He had learned to do that when he was quite young and heedless. He remembered just how he had felt when, after working hard, oh, so hard, to cut a big tree, he had warned all his friends to get out of the way so that they would not be hurt when it fell, and then it hadn't fallen at all because the top had caught in another tree. He was so mortified that he didn't get over it for a long time.

So now he made sure that a tree was going to fall clear and just where he wanted it. Then he sat up on his hind legs, and with his great broad tail for a brace, began to make the chips fly. You know Paddy has the most wonderful teeth for cutting. They are long and broad and sharp. He would begin by making a deep bite, and then another just a little way below. Then he would pry out the little piece of wood between. When he had cut very deep on one side so that the tree would fall that way, he would work around to the other side. Just as soon as the tree began to lean and he was sure that it was going to fall, he would scamper away so as to be out of danger. He loved to see those tall trees lean forward slowly, then faster and faster, till they struck the ground with a crash.

Just as soon as they were down, he would trim off the branches until the trees were just long poles. This was easy work, for he could take off a good-sized branch with one bite. On many he left their bushy tops. When he had trimmed them to suit him and had cut them into the right lengths, he would tug and pull them down to the place where he meant to build his dam.

There he placed the poles side by side, not across the Laughing Brook like a bridge, but with the big ends pointing up the Laughing Brook, which was quite broad but shallow right there. To keep them from floating away, he rolled stones and piled mud on the bushy ends. Clear across on both sides he laid those poles until the water began to rise. Then he dragged more poles and piled them on top of these and wedged short sticks crosswise between them.

And all the time the Laughing

They left Grandfather Frog in the Smiling Pool

Brook was having harder and harder work to run. Its merry laugh grew less merry and finally almost stopped, because, you see, the water could not get through between all those poles and sticks fast enough. It was just about that time that the little people of the Smiling Pool decided that it was time to see just what Paddy was doing, and they started up the Laughing Brook, leaving only Grandfather Frog and the tadpoles in the Smiling Pool, which for a little while would smile no more.

III

Paddy Has Many Visitors

PADDY THE BEAVER knew perfectly well that he would have visitors just as soon as he began to build his dam. He expected a lot of them. You see, he knew that none of them ever had seen a Beaver at work unless perhaps it was Prickly Porky the Porcupine, who also had come down from the North. So as he worked he kept his ears open, and he smiled to himself as he heard a little rustle here and then a little rustle there. He knew just what those little rustles meant. Each one meant another visitor. Yes, Sir, each rustle meant another visitor, and yet not one had shown himself.

Paddy chuckled. "Seems to me that you are dreadfully afraid to show yourselves," said he in a loud voice, just as if he were talking to nobody in particular. Everything was still. There wasn't so much as a rustle after Paddy spoke. He chuckled again. He could just feel ever so many eyes watching him, though he didn't see a single pair. And he knew that the reason his visitors were hiding so carefully was because they were afraid of him. You see, Paddy was much bigger than most of the little meadow and forest people, and they didn't know what kind of a temper he might have. It is always safest to be very distrustful of strangers. That is one of the very first things taught all little meadow and forest children.

Of course, Paddy knew all about this. He had been brought up that way. "Be sure, and then you'll never be sorry" had been

one of his mother's favorite say-
ings, and he had always remembered it. Indeed, it had saved him
a great deal of trouble. So now
he was perfectly willing to go
right on working and let his hidden visitors watch him until they
were sure that he meant them no
harm. You see, he himself felt
quite sure that none of them was
big enough to do him any harm.
Little Joe Otter was the only one
he had any doubts about, and he
felt quite sure that Little Joe
wouldn't try to pick a quarrel.
So he kept right on cutting trees,
trimming off the branches, and
hauling the trunks down to the

dam he was building. Some of them he floated down the Laughing Brook. This was easier.

Now when the little people of the Smiling Pool, who were the first to find out that Paddy the Beaver had come to the Green Forest, had started up the Laughing Brook to see what he was doing, they had told the Merry Little Breezes where they were going. The Merry Little Breezes had been greatly excited. They couldn't understand how a stranger could have been living in the Green Forest without their knowledge. You see, they quite forgot that they very seldom wandered

to the deepest part of the Green
Forest. Of course they started at
once, as fast as they could go, to
tell all the other little people
who live on or around the Green
Meadows, all but Old Man Coyote.
For some reason they thought it
best not to tell him. They were a
little doubtful about Old Man
Coyote. He was so big and strong
and so sly and smart that all his
neighbors were afraid of him.
Perhaps the Merry Little Breezes
had this fact in mind, and knew
that none would dare go to call
on the stranger if they knew that
Old Man Coyote was going too.
Anyway, they simply passed the

time of day with Old Mr. Coyote and hurried on to tell everyone else, and the very last one they met was Sammy Jay.

Sammy was terribly put out to think that anything should be going on that he didn't know about first. You know he is very fond of prying into the affairs of other people, and he loves dearly to boast that there is nothing going on in the Green Forest or on the Green Meadows that he doesn't know about. So now his pride was hurt, and he was in a terrible rage as he started after the Merry Little Breezes for the place deep in the Green Forest where they said Paddy the Beaver was at work. He didn't believe a word of it, but he would see for himself.

Sammy Jay Speaks His Mind

WHEN Sammy Jay reached the place deep in the Green Forest where Paddy the Beaver was so hard at work, he didn't hide as had the little four-footed people. You see, of course, he had no reason to hide, because he felt perfectly safe. Paddy had just cut a big tree, and it fell with a crash as Sammy came hur-

rying up. Sammy was so surprised
that for a minute he couldn't
find his tongue. He had not supposed that anybody but Farmer
Brown or Farmer Brown's boy
could cut down so large a tree as
that, and it quite took his breath
away. But he got it again in a
minute. He was boiling with
anger, anyway, to think that he
should have been the last to learn
that Paddy had come down from
the North to make his home in
the Green Forest, and here was a
chance to speak his mind.

"Thief! thief! thief!" he
screamed in his harshest voice.

Paddy the Beaver looked up

with a twinkle in his eyes. "Hello, Mr. Jay! I see you haven't any better manners than your cousin who lives up where I came from," said he.

"Thief! thief! thief!" screamed Sammy, hopping up and down, he was so angry.

"Meaning yourself, I suppose," said Paddy. "I never did see an honest Jay, and I don't suppose I ever will."

"Ha, ha, ha!" laughed Peter Rabbit, who had quite forgotten that he was hiding.

"Oh, how do you do, Mr. Rabbit? I'm very glad you have called on me this morning," said Paddy, just as if he hadn't known all the time just where Peter was. "Mr. Jay seems to have gotten out of the wrong side of his bed this morning."

Peter laughed again. "He always does," said he. "If he didn't, he wouldn't be happy. You wouldn't think it to look at him, but he is happy right now. He doesn't know it, but he is. He always is happy when he can show what a bad temper he has."

Sammy Jay glared down at Peter. Then he glared at Paddy. And all the time he still shrieked "Thief!" as hard as ever he could. Paddy kept right on working, pay-

Sammy Jay glared down at Peter, then he glared at Paddy

ing no attention to Sammy. This made Sammy more angry than ever. He kept coming nearer and nearer until at last he was in the very tree that Paddy happened to be cutting. Paddy's eyes twinkled.

"I'm no thief!" he exclaimed suddenly.

"You are! You are! Thief! Thief!" shrieked Sammy. "You're stealing our trees!"

"They're not your trees," retorted Paddy. "They belong to the Green Forest, and the Green Forest belongs to all who love it, and we all have a perfect right to take what we need from it. I need these trees, and I've just as much right to take them as you have to take the fat acorns that drop in the fall."

"No such thing!" screamed Sammy. You know he can't talk without screaming, and the more excited he gets, the louder he screams. "No such thing! Acorns are food. They are meant to eat. I have to have them to live. But you are cutting down whole trees. You are spoiling the Green Forest. You don't belong here. Nobody invited you, and nobody wants you. You're a thief!"

Then up spoke Jerry Muskrat, who, you know, is cousin to Paddy the Beaver.

"Don't you mind him," said he, pointing at Sammy Jay. "Nobody does. He's the greatest trouble-maker in the Green Forest or on the Green Meadows. He would steal from his own relatives. Don't mind what he says, Cousin Paddy."

Now all this time Paddy had been working away just as if no one was around. Just as Jerry stopped speaking, Paddy thumped the ground with his tail, which is his way of warning people to watch out, and suddenly scurried away as fast as he could run. Sammy Jay was so surprised that he couldn't find his tongue for a

[*31*]

minute, and he didn't notice anything peculiar about that tree. Then suddenly he felt himself falling. With a frightened scream, he spread his wings to fly, but branches of the tree swept him down with them right into the Laughing Brook.

You see, while Sammy had been speaking his mind, Paddy the Beaver had cut down the very tree in which he was sitting.

Sammy wasn't hurt, but he was wet and muddy and terribly frightened—the most miserable-looking Jay that ever was seen. It was too much for all the little people who were hiding. They just had to laugh. Then they all came out to pay their respects to Paddy the Beaver.

V

Paddy Keeps
His Promise

PADDY THE BEAVER kept right
on working just as if he
hadn't any visitors. You see, it is
a big undertaking to build a dam.
And when that was done there
was a house to build and a supply of food for the winter to cut
and store. Oh, Paddy the Beaver
had no time for idle gossip, you
may be sure! So he kept right on

[*34*]

building his dam. It didn't look much like a dam at first, and some of Paddy's visitors turned up their noses when they first saw it. They had heard stories of what a wonderful dam-builder Paddy was, and they had expected to see something like the smooth, grass-covered bank with which Farmer Brown kept the Big River from running back on his low lands. Instead, all they saw was a great pile of poles and sticks which looked like anything but a dam.

"Pooh!" exclaimed Billy Mink, "I guess we needn't worry about the Laughing Brook and the

Smiling Pool, if that is the best Paddy can do. Why, the water of the Laughing Brook will work through that in no time."

Of course Paddy heard him, but he said nothing, just kept right on working.

"Just look at the way he has laid those sticks!" continued Billy Mink. "Seems as if anyone would know enough to lay them across the Laughing Brook instead of just the other way. I could build a better dam than that."

Paddy said nothing; he just kept right on working.

"Yes, Sir," Billy boasted. "I could build a better dam than

that. Why, that pile of sticks will never stop the water."

"Is something the matter with your eyesight, Billy Mink?" inquired Jerry Muskrat.

"Of course not!" retorted Billy indignantly. "Why?"

"Oh, nothing much, only you don't seem to notice that already the Laughing Brook is over its banks above Paddy's dam," replied Jerry, who had been studying the dam with a great deal of interest.

Billy looked a wee bit foolish, for sure enough there was a little pool just above the dam, and it was growing bigger.

[37]

Billy Mink looked a wee bit foolish

Paddy still kept at work, saying nothing. He was digging in front of the dam now, and the mud and grass he dug up he stuffed in between the ends of the sticks and patted down with his hands. He did this all along the front of the dam and on top of it, too, wherever he thought it was needed. Of course this made it harder for the water to work through, and the little pond above the dam began to grow faster. It wasn't a great while before it was nearly to the top of the dam, which at first was very low. Then Paddy brought more sticks. This was easier now, because he could

[*39*]

float them down from where he was cutting. He would put them in place on the top of the dam, then hurry for more. Wherever it was needed, he would put in mud. He even rolled a few stones in to help hold the mass.

So the dam grew and grew, and so did the pond above the dam. Of course, it took a good many days to build so big a dam, and a lot of hard work! Every morning the little people of the Green Forest and the Green Meadows would visit it, and every morning they would find that it had grown a great deal in the night, for that is when Paddy likes best to work.

By this time, the Laughing Brook had stopped laughing, and down in the Smiling Pool there was hardly water enough for the minnows to feel safe a minute. Billy Mink had stopped making fun of the dam, and all the little people who live in the Laughing Brook and the Smiling Pool were terribly worried.

To be sure, Paddy had warned them of what he was going to do, and had promised that as soon as his pond was big enough, the water would once more run in the Laughing Brook. They tried to believe him, but they couldn't help having just a wee bit of fear that he might not be wholly honest. You see, they didn't know him, for he was a stranger. Jerry Muskrat was the only one who seemed absolutely sure that everything would be all right. Perhaps that was because Paddy is his cousin, and Jerry couldn't help feeling proud of such a big cousin and one who was so smart.

So day by day the dam grew, and the pond grew, and then one morning Grandfather Frog, down in what had once been the Smiling Pool, heard a sound that made his heart jump for joy. It was a murmur that kept growing and growing, until at last it was the merry laugh of the Laughing Brook. Then he knew that Paddy had kept his word, and water would once more fill the Smiling Pool.

Farmer Brown's Boy Grows Curious

NOW IT HAPPENED that the very day before Paddy the Beaver decided that his pond was big enough, and so allowed the water to run in the Laughing Brook once more, Farmer Brown's boy took it into his head to go fishing in the Smiling Pool. Just as usual he went whistling down across the Green Meadows. Somehow, when he goes fishing, he always feels like whistling. Grandfather Frog heard him coming and dived into the little bit of water remaining in the Smiling Pool and stirred up the mud at the bottom so that Farmer Brown's boy shouldn't see him.

Nearer and nearer drew the whistle. Suddenly it stopped right short off. Farmer Brown's boy had come in sight of the Smiling Pool or rather, it was what used to be the Smiling Pool. Now there wasn't any Smiling Pool, for the very little pool left was too small and sickly looking to smile. There were great banks of mud, out of which grew the bulrushes. The lily pads were forlornly stretched out toward the tiny pool of water remaining. Where the banks were steep and high, the holes that Jerry Muskrat and Billy Mink knew so well were plain to see. Over at one side stood Jerry Muskrat's house, wholly out of water.

Somehow, it seemed to Farmer Brown's boy that he must be dreaming. He never, never had seen anything like this before, not even in the very driest weather of the hottest part of the summer. He looked this way and looked that way. The Green Meadows looked just as usual. The Green Forest looked just as usual. The Laughing Brook—ha! What was the matter with the Laughing Brook? He couldn't hear it and that, you know, was very unusual. He dropped his rod and ran over to the Laughing Brook. There wasn't any brook. No, sir, there wasn't any brook; just pools of water with the tiniest of streams trickling between. Big stones over which he had always seen the water running in the prettiest of little white falls were bare and dry. In the little pools frightened minnows were darting about.

Farmer Brown's boy scratched

his head in a puzzled way. "I don't understand it," said he. "I don't understand it at all. Something must have gone wrong with the springs that supply the water for the Laughing Brook. They must have failed. Yes, Sir, that is just what must have happened. But I never heard of such a thing happening before, and I really don't see how it could happen." He stared up into the Green Forest just as if he thought he could see those springs. Of course, he didn't think anything of the kind. He was just turning it all over in his mind. "I know what I'll do! I'll go up to those springs this afternoon and find out what the trouble is," he said out loud. "They are way over almost on the other side of the Green Forest, and the easiest way to get there will be to start from home and cut across the Old Pasture up to the edge of the Mountain behind the Green Forest. If I try to follow up the Laughing Brook now, it will take too long, because it winds and twists so. Besides, it is too hard work."

With that, Farmer Brown's boy went back and picked up his rod. Then he started for home across the Green Meadows, and for once he wasn't whistling. You see, he

[49]

Jimmy Skunk just grinned and went on about his business

was too busy thinking. In fact,
he was so busy thinking that he
didn't see Jimmy Skunk until he
almost stepped on him, and then
he gave a frightened jump and
ran, for without a gun he was
just as much afraid of Jimmy as
Jimmy was of him when he did
have a gun.

Jimmy just grinned and went
on about his business. It always
tickles Jimmy to see people run
away from him, especially people
so much bigger than himself;
they look so silly.

"I should think that they
would have learned by this time
that if they don't bother me, I

won't bother them," he muttered, as he rolled over a stone to look for fat beetles. "Somehow, folks never seem to understand me."

Farmer Brown's Boy Gets Another Surprise

ACROSS the Old Pasture to the foot of the Mountain back of the Green Forest tramped Farmer Brown's boy. Ahead of him trotted Bowser the Hound, sniffing and snuffing for the tracks of Reddy or Granny Fox. Of course he didn't find them, for

Reddy and Granny hadn't been up in the Old Pasture for a long time. But he did find old Jed Thumper, the big gray Rabbit who had made things so uncomfortable for Peter Rabbit once upon a time, and gave old Jed such a fright that he didn't look where he was going and almost ran head-first into Farmer Brown's boy.

"Hi, there, you old cottontail!" yelled Farmer Brown's boy, and this frightened old Jed still more, so that he actually ran right past his own castle of bullbriars without seeing it.

Farmer Brown's boy kept on his way, laughing at the fright of old Jed Thumper. Presently he reached the springs from which came the water that made the very beginning of the Laughing Brook. He expected to find them dry, for way down on the Green Meadows the Smiling Pool was nearly dry, and the Laughing Brook was nearly dry, and he had supposed that of course the reason was that the springs where the Laughing Brook started were no longer bubbling.

But they were! The clear cold water came bubbling up out of the ground just as it always had, and ran off down into the Green Forest in a little stream that would grow and grow as it ran and become the Laughing Brook. Farmer Brown's boy took off his ragged old straw hat and scowled down at the bubbling water just as if he thought it had no business to be bubbling there.

Of course, he didn't think just that. The fact is, he didn't know just what he did think. Here were the springs bubbling away just as they always had. There was the little stream starting off down into the Green Forest with a gurgle that by and by would become a laugh, just as it always had. And yet down on the Green Meadows on the other side of the

Green Forest there was no longer a Laughing Brook or a Smiling Pool. He felt as if he ought to pinch himself to make sure that he was awake and not dreaming.

"I don't know what it means," said he, talking out loud. "No, Sir, I don't know what it means at all, but I'm going to find out. There's a cause for everything in this world, and when a fellow doesn't know a thing, it is his business to find out all about it. I'm going to find out what has happened to the Laughing Brook, if it takes me a year!"

With that he started to follow the little stream which ran gurgling down into the Green Forest. He had followed that little stream more than once, and now he found it just as he remembered it. The farther it ran, the larger it grew, until at last it became the Laughing Brook, merrily tumbling over rocks and making deep pools in which the trout loved to hide. At last he came to the edge of a little open hollow in the very heart of the Green Forest. He knew what splendid deep holes there were in the Laughing Brook here, and how the big trout loved to lie in them because they were deep and cool. He was thinking of these trout now and wishing that he had brought along his fishing rod. He pushed his way through a thicket of alders and then—Farmer Brown's boy stopped suddenly and fairly gasped! He had to stop because there right in front of him was a pond!

He rubbed his eyes and looked again. Then he stooped down and put his hand in the water to see if it was real. There was no doubt about it. It was real water—a real pond where there never had been a pond before. It was very still there in the heart of the Green Forest. It was always very still there, but it seemed stiller than usual as he tramped around the edge of this strange pond. He felt as if it were all a dream. He wondered if pretty soon he wouldn't wake up and find it all untrue. But he didn't, and so he kept on tramping until presently he came to a dam—a splendid dam of logs and sticks and mud. Over the top of it the water was running, and down in the Green Forest below he could hear the Laughing Brook just beginning to laugh once more. Farmer Brown's boy sat down with his elbows on his knees and his chin in his hands. He was almost too much surprised to even think.

VIII

Peter Rabbit Gets
a Ducking

FARMER BROWN'S boy sat with his chin in his hands staring at the new pond in the Green Forest and at the dam which had made it. That dam puzzled him. Who could have built it? What did they build it for? Why hadn't he heard them chopping? He looked carelessly at the stump of one of the trees, and then a still more puzzled look made deep furrows between his eyes. It looked—yes, it looked very much as if teeth, and not an axe, had cut down that tree. Farmer Brown's boy stared and stared, his mouth gaping wide open. He looked so funny that Peter Rabbit, who was hiding under an old pile of brush close by, nearly laughed right out.

But Peter didn't laugh. No, Sir, Peter didn't laugh, for just that very minute something happened. Sniff! Sniff! That was right behind him at the very edge of the old brushpile, and every hair on Peter stood on end with fright.

"Bow, wow, wow!" It seemed to Peter that the great voice was right in his very ears. It frightened him so that he just had to jump. He didn't have time to think. And so he jumped right out from under the pile of brush and of course right into plain sight. And the very instant he jumped there came another great roar behind him. Of course it was from Bowser the Hound. You see, Bowser had been following the trail of his master, but as he always stops to sniff at everything he passes, he had been some dis-

No, indeed, it wasn't the best of going

tance behind. When he came to the pile of brush under which Peter was hiding he had sniffed at that, and of course he had smelled Peter right away.

Now when Peter jumped out so suddenly, he had landed right at one end of the dam. The second roar of Bowser's great voice frightened him still more, and he jumped right up on the dam. There was nothing for him to do now but go across, and it wasn't the best of going. No, indeed, it wasn't the best of going. You see, it was mostly a tangle of sticks. Happy Jack Squirrel or Chatterer the Red Squirrel or Striped Chipmunk would have skipped across it without the least trouble. But Peter Rabbit has no sharp little claws with which to cling to logs and sticks, and right away he was in a peck of trouble. He slipped down between the sticks, scrambled out, slipped again, and then, trying to make a long jump, he lost his balance and—tumbled heels over head into the water!

Poor Peter Rabbit! He gave himself up for lost this time. He could swim, but at best he is a poor swimmer and doesn't like the water. He couldn't dive and keep out of sight like Jerry Muskrat or Billy Mink. All he could do was to paddle as fast as his legs would go. The water had gone up his nose and down his throat so that he choked, and all the time he felt sure that Bowser the Hound would plunge in after him and catch him. And if he shouldn't, why Farmer Brown's boy would simply wait for him to come ashore and then catch him.

But Farmer Brown's boy didn't do anything of the kind. No, Sir, he didn't. Instead he shouted to Bowser and called him away. Bowser didn't want to come, but he long ago learned to obey, and very slowly he walked

over to where his master was sitting.
"You know it wouldn't be fair,
old fellow, to try to catch Peter
now. It wouldn't be fair at all,
and we never want to do anything unfair, do we?" said he.
Perhaps Bowser didn't agree, but
he wagged his tail as if he did,
and sat down beside his master
to watch Peter swim.

It seemed to Peter as if he
never, never would reach the
shore, though really it was only
a very little distance that he had
to swim. When he did scramble
out, he was a sorry-looking Rabbit. He didn't waste any time,
but started for home as fast as

he could go, lipperty-lipperty-lip. And Farmer Brown's boy and Bowser the Hound just laughed and didn't try to catch him at all.

"Well, I never!" exclaimed Sammy Jay, who had seen it all from the top of a pine tree. "Well, I never! I guess Farmer Brown's boy isn't so bad, after all."

Paddy Plans a House

PADDY THE BEAVER sat on his dam, and his eyes shone with happiness as he looked out over the shining water of the pond he had made. All around the edge of it grew the tall trees of the Green Forest. It was very beautiful and very still and very lonesome. That is, it would have seemed lonesome to almost anyone but Paddy the Beaver. But

Paddy never is lonesome. You see, he finds company in the trees and flowers and all the little plants.

It was still, very, very still. Over on one side was a beautiful rosy glow in the water. It was the reflection from jolly, round, red Mr. Sun. Paddy couldn't see him because of the tall trees, but he knew exactly what Mr. Sun was doing. He was going to bed behind the Purple Hills. Pretty soon the little stars would come out and twinkle down at him. He loves the little stars and always watches for the first one.

Yes, Paddy the Beaver was very

happy. He would have been perfectly happy but for one thing:
Farmer Brown's boy had found his
dam and pond that very afternoon, and Paddy wasn't quite
sure what Farmer Brown's boy
might do. He had kept himself
snugly hidden while Farmer
Brown's boy was there, and he
felt quite sure that Farmer
Brown's boy didn't know who
had built the dam. But for this
reason he might, he just might,
try to find out all about it, and
that would mean that Paddy
would have to be always on the
watch.

"But what's the use of worrying over troubles that haven't come yet, and may never come? Time enough to worry when they do come," said Paddy to himself, which shows that Paddy has a great deal of wisdom in his little brown head. "The thing for me to do now is to get ready for winter, and that means a great deal of work," he continued. "Let me see, I've got to build a house, a big, stout, warm house, where I will be warm and safe when my pond is frozen over. And I've got to lay in a supply of food, enough to last me until gentle Sister South Wind comes to prepare the way for lovely Mistress

Spring. My, my, I can't afford to be sitting here dreaming, when there is such a lot to be done!"

With that Paddy slipped into the water and swam all around his new pond to make sure of just the best place to build his house. Now, placing one's house in just the right place is a very important matter. Some people are dreadfully careless about this. Jimmy Skunk, for instance, often makes the mistake of digging his house (you know Jimmy makes his house underground) right where everyone who happens along that way will see it. Perhaps that is because Jimmy is so

[*74*]

independent that he doesn't care who knows where he lives.

But Paddy the Beaver never is careless. He always chooses just the very best place. He makes sure that it is best before he begins. So now, although he was quite positive just where his house should be, he swam around the pond to make doubly sure. Then, when he was quite satisfied, he swam over to the place he had chosen. It was where the water was quite deep.

"There mustn't be the least chance that the ice will ever get thick enough to close up my doorway," said he, "and I'm sure it never will here. I must make the foundations strong and the walls thick. I must have plenty of mud to plaster with, and inside, up above the water, I must have the snuggest, warmest room where I can sleep in comfort. This is the place to build it, and it is high time I was at work."

With that Paddy swam over to the place where he had cut the trees for his dam, and his heart was light, for he had long ago learned that the surest way to be happy is to be busy.

Paddy Starts His House

JERRY MUSKRAT was very much interested when he found that Paddy the Beaver, who, you know, is his cousin, was building a house. Jerry is a house-builder himself, and down deep in his heart he very much doubted if Paddy could build as good a house as he could. His house was

Jerry Muskrat was very much interested

down in the Smiling Pool, and
Jerry thought it a very wonderful
house indeed, and was very proud
of it. It was built of mud and
sod and little alder and willow
twigs and bulrushes. Jerry had
spent one winter in it, and he
had decided to spend another
there after he had fixed it up a
little. So, as long as he didn't
have to build a brand-new house,
he could afford the time to watch
his cousin Paddy. Perhaps he
hoped that Paddy would ask his
advice.

But Paddy did nothing of the
kind. He had seen Jerry Muskrat's house, and he had smiled.

But he had taken great pains not to let Jerry see that smile. He wouldn't have hurt Jerry's feelings for the world. He is too polite and good-natured to do anything like that. So Jerry sat on the end of an old log and watched Paddy work. The first thing to build was the foundation. This was of mud and grass with sticks worked into it to hold it together. Paddy dug the mud from the bottom of his new pond. And because the pond was new, there was a great deal of grassy sod there, which was just what Paddy needed. It was very convenient.

Jerry watched a little while and

[*80*]

then, because Jerry is a worker himself, he just had to get busy and help. Rather timidly he told his big cousin that he would like to have a share in building the new house.

"All right," replied Paddy, "that will be fine. You can bring mud while I am getting the sticks and grass."

So Jerry dived down to the bottom of the pond and dug up mud and piled it on the foundation and was happy. The little stars looked down and twinkled merrily as they watched the two workers. So the foundation grew and grew down under the water.

Jerry was very much surprised at the size of it. It was ever and ever so much bigger than the foundation for his own house. You see, he had forgotten how much bigger Paddy is.

Each night Jerry and Paddy worked, resting during the daytime. Occasionally Bobby Coon or Reddy Fox or Unc' Billy Possum or Jimmy Skunk would come to the edge of the pond to see what was going on. Peter Rabbit came every night. But they couldn't see much because, you know, Paddy and Jerry were working under water.

But at last Peter was rewarded. There, just above the water, was a splendid platform of mud and grass and sticks. A great many sticks were carefully laid as soon as the platform was above the water, for Paddy was very particular about this. You see, it was to be the floor for the splendid room he was planning to build. When it suited him, he began to pile mud in the very middle.

Jerry puzzled and puzzled over this. Where was Paddy's room going to be, if he piled up the mud that way? But he didn't like to ask questions, so he kept right on helping. Paddy would dive down to the bottom and then come up with double handfuls of mud, which he held against his chest. He would scramble out onto the platform and waddle over to the pile in the middle, where he would put the mud and pat it down. Then back to the bottom for more.

And so the mud pile grew and grew, until it was quite two feet high.

"Now," said Paddy, "I'll build the walls, and I guess you can't help me much with those. I'm going to begin them tomorrow night. Perhaps you will like to see me do it, Cousin Jerry."

"I certainly will," replied Jerry, still puzzling over that pile of mud in the middle.

Peter Rabbit and Jerry Muskrat Are Puzzled

JERRY MUSKRAT was more and more sure that his big cousin, Paddy the Beaver, didn't know quite so much as he might about house-building. Jerry would have liked to offer some suggestions, but he didn't quite dare. You see, he was very anxious not to displease his big cousin. But he felt that he simply had got to speak his mind to someone, so he swam across to where he had seen Peter Rabbit almost every night since Paddy began to build. Sure enough, Peter was there, sitting up very straight and staring with big round eyes at the platform of mud and sticks out in the water where Paddy the Beaver was at work.

"Well, Peter, what do you think of it?" asked Jerry.

"What is it?" asked Peter innocently. "Is it another dam?"

Jerry threw back his head and laughed and laughed.

"Is it another dam?" Peter asked

Peter looked at him suspiciously. "I don't see anything to laugh at," said he.

"Why, it's a house, you stupid. It's Paddy's new house," replied Jerry, wiping the tears of laughter from his eyes.

"I'm not stupid!" retorted Peter. "How was I to know that that pile of mud and sticks is meant for a house? It certainly doesn't look it. Where is the door?"

"To tell you the truth, I don't think it is much of a house myself," replied Jerry. "It has got a door, all right. In fact, it has got three. You can't see them be-

cause they are under water, and
there is a passage from each right
up through that platform of mud
and sticks, which is the foundation of the house. It really is a
very fine foundation, Peter; it
really is. But what I can't understand is what Paddy is thinking
of by building that great pile of
mud right in the middle. When
he gets his walls built, where will
his bedroom be? There won't be
any room at all. It won't be a
house at all—just a big useless
pile of sticks and mud."

Peter scratched his head and
then pulled his whiskers thoughtfully as he gazed out at the pile

in the water where Paddy the Beaver was at work.

"It does look foolish, that's a fact," said he. "Why don't you point out to him the mistake he is making, Jerry? You have built such a splendid house yourself that you ought to be able to help Paddy and show him his mistakes."

Jerry had smiled a very self-satisfied smile when Peter mentioned his fine house, but he shook his head at the suggestion that he should give Paddy advice.

"I—I don't just like to," he confessed. "You know, he might not like it and—and it doesn't seem as if it would be quite polite."

Peter sniffed. "That wouldn't trouble me any if he were my cousin," said he.

Jerry shook his head. "No, I don't believe it would," he replied, "but it does trouble me and—and—well, I think I'll wait awhile."

Now all this time Paddy had been hard at work. He was bringing the longest branches which he had cut from the trees out of which he had built his dam, and a lot of slender willow and alder poles. He pushed these ahead of him as he swam. When he reached the foundation of his

[*91*]

house, he would lean them against the pile of mud in the middle with their big ends resting on the foundation. So he worked all the way around until by and by the mud pile in the middle couldn't be seen. It was completely covered with sticks, and they were cunningly fastened together at the tops.

XII

Jerry Muskrat
Learns Something

If you think you know it all
You are riding for a fall.
Use your ears and use your eyes,
But hold your tongue and you'll be wise.

JERRY MUSKRAT will tell you that
is as true as true can be.
Jerry knows. He found it out for
himself. Now he is very careful
what he says about other people
or what they are doing. But he

wasn't so careful when his cousin, Paddy the Beaver, was building his house. No, Sir, Jerry wasn't so careful then. He thought he knew more about building a house than Paddy did. He was sure of it when he watched Paddy heap up a great pile of mud right in the middle where his room ought to be, and then build a wall of sticks around it. He said as much to Peter Rabbit.

Now it is never safe to say anything to Peter Rabbit that you don't care to have others know. Peter has a great deal of respect for Jerry Muskrat's opinion on house-building. You see, he very much admires Jerry's snug house in the Smiling Pool. It really is a very fine house, and Jerry may be excused for being proud of it. But that doesn't excuse Jerry for thinking that he knows all there is to know about house-building. Of course Peter told everyone he met that Paddy the Beaver was making a foolish mistake in building his house, and that Jerry Muskrat, who ought to know, said so.

So whenever they got the chance, the little people of the Green Forest and the Green Meadows would steal up to the shore of Paddy's new pond and chuckle as they looked out at the great pile of sticks and mud which Paddy had built for a house, but in which he had forgotten to make a room. At least they supposed that he had forgotten this very important thing. He must have, for there wasn't any room. It was a great joke. They laughed a lot about it, and they lost a great deal of the respect for Paddy which they had had since he built his wonderful dam.

Jerry and Peter sat in the moonlight talking it over. Paddy had stopped bringing sticks for his wall. He had dived down out of sight, and he was gone a long time. Suddenly Jerry noticed that the water had grown very, very muddy all around Paddy's new house. He wrinkled his brows trying to think what Paddy could be doing. Presently Paddy came up for air. Then he went down again, and the water grew muddier than ever. This went on for a long time. Every little while Paddy would come up for air and a few minutes of rest. Then down he would go, and the water would grow muddier and muddier.

At last Jerry could stand it no longer. He just had to see what was going on. He slipped into the water and swam over to where the water was muddiest. Just as he got there up came Paddy.

"Hello, Cousin Jerry!" said he. "I was just going to invite you over to see what you think of my house inside. Just follow me."

Paddy dived, and Jerry dived after him. He followed Paddy in at one of the three doorways under water and up a smooth hall right into the biggest, nicest bedroom Jerry had ever seen in all his life. He just gasped in sheer surprise. He couldn't do anything else. He couldn't find his

Paddy dived and Jerry dived after him

tongue to say a word. Here he was in this splendid great room up above the water, and he had been so sure that there wasn't any room at all! He just didn't know what to make of it.

Paddy's eyes twinkled. "Well," said he, "what do you think of it?"

"I—I—think it is splendid, just perfectly splendid! But I don't understand it at all, Cousin Paddy. I—I— Where is that great pile of mud I helped you build in the middle?" Jerry looked as foolish as he felt when he asked this.

"Why, I've dug it all away.

That's what made the water so muddy," replied Paddy.

"But what did you build it for in the first place?" Jerry asked.

"Because I had to have something solid to rest my sticks against while I was building my walls, of course," replied Paddy. "When I got the tops fastened together for a roof, they didn't need a support any longer, and then I dug it away to make this room. I couldn't have built such a big room any other way. I see you don't know very much about house-building, Cousin Jerry."

"I—I'm afraid I don't," confessed Jerry sadly.

XIII

The Queer Storehouse

EVERYBODY knew that Paddy the Beaver was laying up a supply of food for the winter, and everybody thought it was queer food. That is, everybody but Prickly Porky the Porcupine thought so. Prickly Porky likes the same kind of food, but he never lays up a supply. He just goes out and gets it when he wants it, winter or summer. What kind of food was it? Why, bark, to be sure. Yes, Sir, it was just bark—the bark of certain kinds of trees.

Now Prickly Porky can climb the trees and eat the bark right there, but Paddy the Beaver cannot climb, and if he should just eat the bark that he can reach from the ground, it would take such a lot of trees to keep him filled up that he would soon spoil the Green Forest. You know, when the bark is taken off a tree all the way around, the tree dies. That is because all the things that a tree draws out of the ground to make it grow and keep it alive are carried up from the roots in the sap, and the sap cannot go up the tree trunks and into the branches when the bark is taken off, because it is up the inside of the bark that it travels. So when the bark is taken from a tree all the way around the trunk, the tree just starves to death.

Now Paddy the Beaver loves the Green Forest as dearly as you and I do, and perhaps even a little more dearly. You see, it is his home. Besides, Paddy never is wasteful. So he cuts down a tree so that he can get all the bark instead of killing a whole lot of trees for a very little bark, as he might do if he were lazy. There isn't a lazy bone in him— not one. The bark he likes best is from the aspen. When he cannot get that, he will eat the bark from the poplar, the alder, the willow, and even the birch. But he likes the aspen so much better that he will work very hard to get it. Perhaps it tastes better because he does have to work so hard for it.

There were some aspen trees growing right on the edge of the pond Paddy had made in the

Green Forest. These he cut just as he had cut the trees for his dam. As soon as a tree was down, he would cut it into short lengths, and with these swim out to where the water was deep, close to his new house. He took them one by one and carried the first ones to the bottom, where he pushed them into the mud just enough to hold them. Then, as fast as he brought more, he piled them on the first ones. And so the pile grew and grew.

Jerry Muskrat, Peter Rabbit, Bobby Coon, and the other little people of the Green Forest watched him with the greatest interest and curiosity. They couldn't quite make out what he was doing. It was almost as if he were building the foundation for another house.

"What's he doing, Jerry?" demanded Peter, when he could keep still no longer.

"I don't exactly know," replied Jerry. "He said that he was going to lay in a supply of food for the winter, just as I told you, and I suppose that is what he is doing. But I don't quite understand what he is taking it all out into the pond for. I believe I'll go ask him."

"Do, and then come tell us,"

begged Peter, who was growing so curious that he couldn't sit still.

So Jerry swam out to where Paddy was so busy. "Is this your food supply, Cousin Paddy?" he asked.

"Yes," replied Paddy, crawling up on the side of his house to rest. "Yes, this is my food supply. Isn't it splendid?"

"I guess it is," replied Jerry, trying to be polite, "though I like lily roots and clams better. But what are you going to do with it? Where is your storehouse?"

"This pond is my storehouse,"

replied Paddy. "I will make a great pile right here close to my house, and the water will keep it nice and fresh all winter. When the pond is frozen over, all I will have to do is to slip out of one of my doorways down there on the bottom, swim over here and get a stick, and fill my stomach. Isn't it handy?"

A Footprint in
the Mud

VERY early one morning Paddy the Beaver heard Sammy Jay making a terrible fuss over in the aspen trees on the edge of the pond Paddy had made in the Green Forest. Paddy couldn't see because he was inside his house, and it has no window, but he could hear. He wrinkled up his brows thoughtfully.

"Seems to me that Sammy is very much excited this morning," said he, talking to himself, a way he has because he is so much alone. "When he screams like that, Sammy is usually trying to do two things at once—make trouble for somebody and keep somebody else out of trouble; and when you come to think of it, that's rather a funny way of doing. It shows that he isn't all bad, and at the same time he is a long way from being all good. Now, I should say from the sounds that Sammy has discovered Reddy Fox trying to steal up on someone over where my aspen

"Reddy Fox thinks perhaps he can catch Peter Rabbit"

trees are growing. Reddy is afraid of me, but I suspect that he knows that Peter Rabbit has been hanging around here a lot lately, watching me work, and he thinks perhaps he can catch Peter. I shall have to whisper in one of Peter's long ears and tell him to watch out."

After a while he heard Sammy Jay's voice growing fainter and fainter in the Green Forest. Finally he couldn't hear it at all. "Whoever was there has gone away, and Sammy has followed just to torment them," thought Paddy. He was very busy making a bed. He is very particular about his bed, is Paddy the Beaver. He makes it of fine splinters of wood which he splits off with those wonderful great cutting teeth of his. This makes the driest kind of a bed. It requires a great deal of patience and work, but patience is one of the first things a little Beaver learns, and honest work well done is one of the greatest pleasures in the world, as Paddy long ago found out for himself. So he kept at work on his bed for some time after all was still outside.

At last Paddy decided that he would go over to his aspen trees and look them over to decide which ones he would cut the next night. He slid down one of his long halls, out the doorway at the bottom of the pond, and then swam up to the surface, where he floated for a few minutes with just his head out of water. And all the time his eyes and nose and ears were busy looking, smelling, and listening for any sign of danger. Everything was still. Sure that he was quite safe, Paddy swam across to the place where the aspen trees grew, and waddled out on the shore.

Paddy looked this way and looked that way. He looked up

in the treetops, and he looked
off up the hill, but most of all he
looked at the ground. Yes, Sir,
Paddy just studied the ground.
You see, he hadn't forgotten the
fuss Sammy Jay had been making
there, and he was trying to find
out what it was all about. At
first he didn't see anything unusual, but by and by he happened to notice a little wet place,
and right in the middle of it was
something that made Paddy's eyes
open wide. It was a footprint!
Someone had carelessly stepped in
the mud.

"Ha!" exclaimed Paddy, and
the hair on his back lifted ever

so little, and for a minute he had a prickly feeling all over. The footprint was very much like that of Reddy Fox, only it was larger.

"Ha!" said Paddy again. "That certainly is the footprint of Old Man Coyote! I see I have got to watch out more sharply than I had thought for. All right, Mr. Coyote; now that I know you are about, you'll have to be smarter than I think you are to catch me. You certainly will be back here tonight looking for me, so I think I'll do my cutting right now in the daytime."

Sammy Jay Makes Paddy a Call

PADDY THE BEAVER was hard at work. He had just cut down a good-sized aspen tree and now he was gnawing it into short lengths to put in his food pile in the pond. As he worked, Paddy was doing a lot of thinking about the footprint of Old Man Coyote in a little patch of mud, for he knew that meant that Old Man Coyote had discovered his pond, and would be hanging around, hoping to catch Paddy off his guard. Paddy knew it just as well as if Old Man Coyote had told him so. That was why he was at work cutting his food supply in the daytime. Usually he works at night, and he knew that Old Man Coyote knew it.

"He'll try to catch me then," thought Paddy, "so I'll do my working on land now and fool him."

The tree he was cutting began to sway and crack. Paddy cut out one more big chip, then hurried away to a safe place while the tree fell with a crash.

"Thief! thief! thief!" screamed a voice just back of Paddy.

"Hello, Sammy Jay! I see you don't feel any better than usual this morning," said Paddy. "Don't you want to sit up in this tree while I cut it down?"

Sammy grew black in the face with anger, for he knew that Paddy was laughing at him. You remember how only a few days before he had been so intent on calling Paddy bad names that he actually hadn't noticed that Paddy was cutting the very tree in which he was sitting, and so when it

[*120*]

fell he had had a terrible fright.

"You think you are very smart, Mr. Beaver, but you'll think differently one of these fine days!" screamed Sammy. "If you knew what I know, you wouldn't be so well satisfied with yourself."

"What do you know?" asked Paddy, pretending to be very much alarmed.

"I'm not going to tell you what I know," retorted Sammy Jay. "You'll find out soon enough. And when you do find out, you'll never steal another tree from our Green Forest. Somebody is going to catch you, and it isn't Farmer Brown's boy either!"

Paddy pretended to be terribly frightened. "Oh, who is it? Please tell me, Mr. Jay," he begged.

Now to be called Mr. Jay made Sammy feel very important. Nearly everybody else called him Sammy. He swelled himself out trying to look as important as he felt, and his eyes snapped with pleasure. He was actually making Paddy the Beaver afraid. At least, he thought he was.

"No, Sir, I won't tell you," he replied. "I wouldn't be you for a great deal, though! Somebody who is smarter than you are is going to catch you, and when he gets through with you, there won't

Paddy pretended to be terribly frightened

be anything left but a few bones. No, Sir, nothing but a few bones!"

"Oh, Mr. Jay, this is terrible news! Whatever am I to do?" cried Paddy, all the time keeping on at work cutting another tree.

"There's nothing you can do," replied Sammy, grinning wickedly at Paddy's fright. "There's nothing you can do unless you go right straight back to the North where you came from. You think you are very smart, but—"

Sammy didn't finish. Crack! Over fell the tree Paddy had been cutting and the top of it fell straight into the alder in which Sammy was sitting. "Oh! Oh!

Help!" shrieked Sammy, spreading his wings and flying away just in time.

Paddy sat down and laughed until his sides ached. "Come make me another call someday, Sammy!" he said. "And when you do, please bring some real news. I know all about Old Man Coyote. You can tell him for me that when he is planning to catch people he should be careful not to leave footprints to give himself away."

Sammy didn't reply. He just sneaked off through the Green Forest, looking quite as foolish as he felt.

XVI

Old Man Coyote Is Very Crafty

Coyote has a crafty brain;
His wits are sharp his ends to gain.

THERE is nothing in the world more true than that. Old Man Coyote has the craftiest brain of all the little people of the Green Forest or the Green Meadows. Sharp as are the wits of old Granny Fox, they are not quite so sharp as the wits of Old Man

Coyote. If you want to fool him, you will have to get up very early in the morning, and then it is more than likely that you will be the one fooled, not he. There is very little going on around him that he doesn't know about. But once in a while something escapes him. The coming of Paddy the Beaver to the Green Forest was one of these things. He didn't know a thing about Paddy until Paddy had finished his dam and his house, and was cutting his supply of food for the winter.

You see, it was this way: When the Merry Little Breezes of Old

Mother West Wind first heard what was going on in the Green Forest and hurried around over the Green Meadows and through the Green Forest to spread the news, as is their way, they took the greatest pains not to even hint it to Old Man Coyote because they were afraid that he would make trouble and perhaps drive Paddy away. The place that Paddy had chosen to build his dam was so deep in the Green Forest that Old Man Coyote seldom went that way. So it was that he knew nothing about Paddy, and Paddy knew nothing about him for some time.

But after a while Old Man

Coyote noticed that the little people of the Green Meadows were not about as much as usual. They seemed to have a secret of some kind. He mentioned the matter to his friend, Digger the Badger.

Digger had been so intent on his own affairs that he hadn't noticed anything unusual, but when Old Man Coyote mentioned the matter he remembered that Blacky the Crow headed straight for the Green Forest every morning. Several times he had seen Sammy Jay flying in the same direction as if in a great hurry to get somewhere.

Old Man Coyote grinned.

He mentioned the matter to Digger the Badger

"That's all I need to know, friend
Digger," said he. "When Blacky
the Crow and Sammy Jay visit a
place more than once, something
interesting is going on there. I
think I'll take a stroll up through
the Green Forest and have a look
around."

With that, off Old Man Coyote
started. But he was too sly and
crafty to go straight to the Green
Forest. He pretended to hunt
around over the Green Meadows
just as he usually did, all the
time working nearer and nearer
to the Green Forest. When he
reached the edge of it, he slipped
in among the trees, and when he

felt that no one was likely to see him, he began to run this way and that way with his nose to the ground.

"Ha!" he exclaimed presently, "Reddy Fox has been this way lately."

Pretty soon he found another trail. "So," said he, "Peter Rabbit has been over here a good deal of late, and his trail goes in the same direction as that of Reddy Fox. I guess all I have to do now is to follow Peter's trail, and it will lead me to what I want to find out."

So Old Man Coyote followed Peter's trail, and he presently

came to the pond of Paddy the Beaver. "Ha!" said he, as he looked out and saw Paddy's new house. "So there is a newcomer to the Green Forest! I have always heard that Beaver is very good eating. My stomach begins to feel empty this very minute." His mouth began to water, and a fierce, hungry look shone in his eyes.

It was just then that Sammy Jay saw him and began to scream at the top of his lungs so that Paddy the Beaver over in his house heard him. Old Man Coyote knew that it was of no use to stay longer with Sammy Jay about, so he took a hasty look at the pond and found where Paddy came ashore to cut his food. Then, shaking his fist at Sammy Jay, he started straight back for the Green Meadows. "I'll just pay a visit here in the night," said he, "and give Mr. Beaver a surprise while he is at work."

But with all his craft, Old Man Coyote didn't notice that he left a footprint in the mud.

XVII

Old Man Coyote Is Disappointed

OLD MAN COYOTE lay stretched out in his favorite napping place on the Green Meadows. He was thinking of what he had found out up in the Green Forest that morning—that Paddy the Beaver was living there. Old Man Coyote's thoughts seemed very pleasant to himself, though really they were very dreadful thoughts. You see, he was thinking how easy it was going to be to catch Paddy the Beaver, and what a splendid meal he would make. He licked his chops at the thought.

"He doesn't know I know he's here," thought Old Man Coyote. "In fact, I don't believe he even knows that I am anywhere around. Of course he won't be watching for me. He cuts his trees at night, so all I will have to do is to hide right close by where he is at work, and he'll walk right into my mouth. Sammy Jay knows I was up there this morning, but Sammy sleeps at night, so he will not give the alarm. My, my, how good that Beaver will taste!" He licked his chops once more, then yawned and closed his eyes for a nap.

Old Man Coyote waited until jolly, round, red Mr. Sun had gone to bed behind the Purple Hills, and the Black Shadows had crept out across the Green Meadows. Then, keeping in the blackest of them, and looking very much like a shadow himself, he slipped into the Green Forest. It was dark in there, and he made straight for Paddy's new pond, trotting along swiftly without making a sound. When he was near the aspen trees which he knew Paddy was planning to cut, he crept forward very slowly and carefully. Everything was still as still could be.

"Good!" thought Old Man Coyote. "I am here first, and now all I need do is to hide and wait for Paddy to come ashore."

So he stretched himself flat behind some brush close beside the little path Paddy had made up from the edge of the water and waited. It was very still, so still that it seemed almost as if he could hear his heart beat. He could see the little stars twinkling

in the sky and their own reflec-
tions twinkling back at them from
the water of Paddy's pond. Old
Man Coyote waited and waited.
He is very patient when there is
something to gain by it. For
such a splendid dinner as Paddy
the Beaver would make, he felt
that he could well afford to be
patient. So he waited and waited,
and everything was as still as if
no living thing but the trees
were there. Even the trees seemed
to be asleep.

At last, after a long, long time,
he heard just the faintest splash.
He pricked up his ears and
peeped out on the pond with the

hungriest look in his yellow eyes. There was a little line of silver coming straight toward him. He knew that it was made by Paddy the Beaver swimming. Nearer and nearer it drew. Old Man Coyote chuckled way down deep inside, without making a sound. He could see Paddy's head now, and Paddy was coming straight in, as if he hadn't a fear in the world.

Almost to the edge of the pond swam Paddy. Then he stopped. In a few minutes he began to swim again, but this time it was back in the direction of his house, and he seemed to be carrying something. It was one of the little food logs he had cut that day, and he was taking it out to his storehouse. Then back he came for another. And so he kept on, never once coming ashore. Old Man Coyote waited until Paddy had carried the last log to his storehouse and then, with a loud whack on the water with his broad tail, had dived and disappeared in his house.

Then Old Man Coyote arose and started elsewhere to look for his dinner, and in his heart was bitter disappointment.

XVIII

Old Man Coyote
Tries Another Plan

FOR three nights Old Man Coyote had stolen up through the Green Forest with the coming of the Black Shadows and had hidden among the aspen trees where Paddy the Beaver cut his food, and for three nights Paddy had failed to come ashore. Each night he had seemed to have enough food logs in the water to keep him busy without cutting more. Old Man Coyote lay there, and the hungry look in his eyes changed to one of doubt and then to suspicion. Could it be that Paddy the Beaver was smarter than he thought? It began to look very much as if Paddy knew perfectly well that he was hiding there each night. Yes, Sir, that's the way it looked. For three nights Paddy hadn't cut a single tree, and yet each night he had plenty of food logs ready to take to his storehouse in the pond.

"That means that he comes ashore in the daytime and cuts

his trees," thought Old Man Coyote as, tired and with black anger in his heart, he trotted home the third night. "He couldn't have found out about me himself; he isn't smart enough. It must be that someone has told him. And nobody knows that I have been over there but Sammy Jay. It must be he who has been the tattletale. I think I'll visit Paddy by daylight tomorrow, and then we'll see!"

Now the trouble with some smart people is that they are never able to believe that others may be as smart as they. Old Man Coyote didn't know that the first time he had visited Paddy's pond he had left behind him a footprint in a little patch of soft mud. If he had known it, he wouldn't have believed that Paddy would be smart enough to guess what that footprint meant. So Old Man Coyote laid all the blame at the door of Sammy Jay, and that very morning, when Sammy came flying over the Green Meadows, Old Man Coyote accused him of being a tattletale and threatened the most dreadful things to Sammy if ever he caught him.

Now Sammy had flown down to the Green Meadows to tell

Old Man Coyote how Paddy was doing all his work on land in the daytime. But when Old Man Coyote began to call him a tattle-tale and accuse him of having warned Paddy, and to threaten dreadful things, he straightway forgot all his anger at Paddy and turned it all on Old Man Coyote. He called him everything he could think of, and this was a great deal, for Sammy has a wicked tongue. When he hadn't any breath left, he flew over to the Green Forest, and there he hid where he could watch all that was going on.

That afternoon Old Man Coyote tried his new plan. He slipped into the Green Forest, looking this way and that way to be sure that no one saw him. Then very, very softly, he crept up through the Green Forest toward the pond of Paddy the Beaver. As he drew near, he heard a crash, and it made him smile. He knew what it meant. It meant that Paddy was at work cutting down trees. With his stomach almost on the ground, he crept forward little by little, little by little, taking the greatest care not to rustle so much as a leaf. Presently he reached a place where he could see the aspen trees, and there, sure enough, was Paddy, sitting up on his hind legs and hard at work cutting another tree.

Old Man Coyote lay down for a few minutes to watch. Then he wriggled a little nearer. Slowly and carefully he drew his legs under him and made ready for a rush. Paddy the Beaver was his at last! At just that very minute a harsh scream rang out right over his head:

"Thief! thief! thief!"

It was Sammy Jay, who had followed him all the way. Paddy the Beaver didn't stop to even look around. He knew what that meant, and he scrambled down his little path to the water as he never had scrambled before. And as he dived with a great splash, Old Man Coyote landed with a great jump on the very edge of the pond.

Paddy and Sammy Jay Become Friends

PADDY THE BEAVER floated in his pond and grinned in the most provoking way at Old Man Coyote, who had so nearly caught him. Old Man Coyote fairly danced with anger on the bank. He had felt so sure of Paddy that time that it was hard work to believe that Paddy had really gotten away from him. He bared his long, cruel teeth, and he looked very fierce and ugly.

"Come on in; the water's fine!" called Paddy.

Now, of course, this wasn't a nice thing for Paddy to do, for it only made Old Man Coyote all the angrier. You see, Paddy knew perfectly well that he was absolutely safe, and he just couldn't resist the temptation to say some unkind things. He had had to be on the watch for days lest he should be caught, and so he hadn't been able to work quite so well as he could have done with nothing to fear, and he still had a lot of preparations to make

"Come on in; the water's fine!" called Paddy

for winter. So he told Old Man
Coyote just what he thought of
him, and that he wasn't as smart
as he thought he was or he never
would have left a footprint in the
mud to give him away.

When Sammy Jay, who was
listening and chuckling as he
listened, heard that, he flew down
where he would be just out of
reach of Old Man Coyote, and
then he just turned that tongue
of his loose, and you know that
some people say that Sammy's
tongue is hung in the middle and
wags at both ends. Of course this
isn't really so, but when he gets
to abusing people it seems as if

it must be true. He called Old Man Coyote every bad name he could think of. He called him a sneak, a thief, a coward, a bully, and a lot of other things.

"You said I had warned Paddy that you were trying to catch him and that was why you failed to find him at work at night, and all the time you had warned him yourself!" screamed Sammy. "I used to think that you were smart, but I know better now. Paddy is twice as smart as you are.

"Mr. Coyote is ever so sly;
Mr. Coyote is clever and spry;
If you believe all you hear.

Mr. Coyote is naught of the kind;
Mr. Coyote is stupid and blind;
   He can't catch a flea on his ear."

Paddy the Beaver laughed till the tears came at Sammy's foolish verse, but it made Old Man Coyote angrier than ever. He was angry with Paddy for escaping from him, and he was angry with Sammy, terribly angry, and the worst of it was he couldn't catch either one, for one was at home in the water and the other was at home in the air and he couldn't follow in either place. Finally he saw it was of no use to stay there to be laughed at, so, muttering and grumbling, he started for the Green Meadows.

As soon as he was out of sight Paddy turned to Sammy Jay.

"Mr. Jay," said he, knowing how it pleased Sammy to be called mister, "Mr. Jay, you have done me a mighty good turn to-day, and I am not going to forget it. You can call me what you please and scream at me all you please, but you won't get any satisfaction out of it, because I simply won't get angry. I will say to myself, 'Mr. Jay saved my life the other day,' and then I won't mind your tongue."

Now this made Sammy feel very proud and very happy. You

[*156*]

know it is very seldom that he hears anything nice said of him. He flew down on the stump of one of the trees Paddy had cut. "Let's be friends," said he.

"With all my heart!" replied Paddy.

Sammy Jay Offers To Help Paddy

PADDY sat looking thoughtfully at the aspen trees he would have to cut to complete his store of food for the winter. All those near the edge of his pond had been cut. The others were scattered about some little distance away. "I don't know," said Paddy out loud. "I don't know."

"What don't you know?" asked

Sammy Jay, who, now that he and Paddy had become friends, was very much interested in what Paddy was doing.

"Why," replied Paddy, "I don't know just how I am going to get those trees. Now that Old Man Coyote is watching for me, it isn't safe for me to go very far from my pond. I suppose I could dig a canal up to some of the nearest trees and then float them down to the pond, but it is hard to work and keep watch for enemies at the same time. I guess I'll have to be content with some of these alders growing close to the water, but the bark of aspens is so much better that I—I wish I could get them."

"What's a canal?" asked Sammy abruptly.

"A canal? Why, a canal is a kind of ditch in which water can run," replied Paddy.

Sammy nodded. "I've seen Farmer Brown dig one over on the Green Meadows, but it looked like a great deal of work. I didn't suppose that anyone else could do it. Do you really mean that you can dig a canal, Paddy?"

"Of course I mean it," replied Paddy, in a surprised tone of voice. "I have helped dig lots of canals. You ought to see some of them back where I came from."

"I'd like to," replied Sammy. "I think it is perfectly wonderful. I don't see how you do it."

"It's easy enough when you know how," replied Paddy. "If I dared to, I'd show you."

Sammy had a sudden idea. It almost made him gasp. "I tell you what, you work and I'll keep watch!" he cried. "You know my eyes are very sharp."

"Will you?" cried Paddy eagerly. "That would be perfectly splendid. You have the sharpest eyes of anyone whom I know, and I would feel perfectly safe with you on watch. But I don't want to put you to all that trouble, Mr. Jay."

"Of course I will," replied Sammy, "and it won't be any trouble at all. I'll just love to do it." You see, it made Sammy feel very proud to have Paddy say that he had such sharp eyes. "When will you begin?"

"Right away, if you will just take a look around and see that it is perfectly safe for me to come out on land."

Sammy didn't wait to hear more. He spread his beautiful blue wings and started off over the Green Forest straight for the Green Meadows. Paddy watched

Sammy didn't wait to hear more

him go with a puzzled and disappointed air. "That's funny,"
thought he. "I thought he really
meant it, and now off he goes
without even saying good-by."

In a little while back came
Sammy, all out of breath. "It's
all right," he panted. "You can
go to work just as soon as you
please."

Paddy looked more puzzled
than ever. "How do you know?"
he asked. "I haven't seen you
looking around."

"I did better than that," replied Sammy. "If Old Man Coyote had been hiding somewhere
in the Green Forest, it might

have taken me some time to find him. But he isn't. You see, I flew straight over to his home in the Green Meadows to see if he is there, and he is. He's taking a sun bath and looking as cross as two sticks. I don't think he'll be back here this morning, but I'll keep a sharp watch while you work."

Paddy made Sammy a low bow. "You certainly are smart, Mr. Jay," said he. "I wouldn't have thought of going over to Old Man Coyote's home to see if he was there. I'll feel perfectly safe with you on guard. Now I'll get to work."

Paddy and Sammy Jay Work Together

JERRY MUSKRAT had been home at the Smiling Pool for several days. But he couldn't stay there long. Oh, my, no! He just had to get back to see what his big cousin, Paddy the Beaver, was doing. So as soon as he was sure that everything was all right at the Smiling Pool he hurried back up the Laughing Brook to Paddy's pond, deep in the Green Forest. As soon as he was in sight of it, he looked eagerly for Paddy. At first he didn't see him. Then he stopped and gazed over at the place where Paddy had been cutting aspen trees for food. Something was going **on** there, something queer. He couldn't make it out.

Just then Sammy Jay came flying over.

"What's Paddy doing?" Jerry asked.

Sammy Jay dropped down to the top of an alder tree and fluffed out all his feathers in a very important way. "Oh," said he, "Paddy and I are building something!"

"You! Paddy and you! Ha, ha! Paddy and you building something!" Jerry laughed.

"Yes, me!" snapped Sammy angrily. "That's what I said; Paddy and I are building something."

Jerry had begun to swim across the pond by this time, and Sammy was flying across. "Why don't you tell the truth, Sammy, and say that Paddy is building something and you are making him all the trouble you can?" called Jerry.

Sammy's eyes snapped angrily,

and he darted down at Jerry's little brown head. "It isn't true!" he shrieked. "You ask Paddy if I'm not helping!"

Jerry ducked under water to escape Sammy's sharp bill. When he came up again, Sammy was over in the little grove of aspen trees where Paddy was at work. Then Jerry discovered something. What was it? Why a little water-path led right up to the aspen trees, and there, at the end of the little water-path, was Paddy the Beaver hard at work. He was digging and piling the earth on one side very neatly. In fact, he was making the water-path longer.

Jerry swam right up the little water-path to where Paddy was working. "Good morning, Cousin Paddy," sad he. "What are you doing?"

"Oh," replied Paddy, "Sammy Jay and I are building a canal."

Sammy Jay looked down at Jerry in triumph, and Jerry looked at Paddy as if he thought that he was joking.

"Sammy Jay? What's Sammy Jay got to do about it?" demanded Jerry.

"A whole lot," replied Paddy. "You see, he keeps watch while I work. If he didn't, I couldn't work, and there wouldn't be any

"Sammy Jay and I are building a canal"

canal. Old Man Coyote has been trying to catch me, and I wouldn't dare work on shore if it wasn't that I am sure that the sharpest eyes in the Green Forest are watching for danger."

Sammy Jay looked very much pleased indeed and very proud.

"So you see, it takes both of us to make this canal; I dig while Sammy watches. So we are building it together," concluded Paddy with a twinkle in his eyes.

"I see," said Jerry slowly. Then he turned to Sammy Jay. "I beg your pardon, Sammy," said he. "I do indeed."

"That's all right," replied

Sammy airily. "What do you think of our canal?"

"I think it is wonderful," replied Jerry.

And indeed it was a very fine canal, straight, wide, and deep enough for Paddy to swim in and float his logs out to the pond. Yes, indeed, it was a very fine canal.

XXII

Paddy Finishes His Harvest

"Sharp his tongue and sharp his eyes—
Sammy guards against surprise.
If 'twere not for Sammy Jay
I could do no work today."

WHEN Sammy overheard Paddy the Beaver say that to Jerry Muskrat, it made him swell up all over with pure pride. You see, Sammy is so used to hearing bad things about himself that to hear something nice like that pleased him immensely. He straightway forgot all the mean things he had said to Paddy when he first saw him—how he had called him a thief because he had cut the aspen trees he needed. He forgot all this. He forgot how Paddy had made him the laughingstock of the Green Forest and the Green Meadows by cuting down the very tree in which he had been sitting. He forgot everything but that Paddy had trusted him to keep watch and now was saying nice things about him. He made up his mind that he would deserve all the nice things that Paddy could say, and he thought that Paddy was the finest fellow in the world.

Jerry Muskrat looked doubtful. He didn't trust Sammy, and he took care not to go far from the water when he heard that Old Man Coyote had been hanging around. But Paddy worked away just as if he hadn't a fear in the world.

"The way to make people want to be trusted is to trust them," said he to himself. "If I show Sammy Jay that I don't really trust him, he will think it is of no use to try and will give it up. But if I do trust him, and he knows that I do, he'll be the best watchman in the Green Forest."

And this shows that Paddy the Beaver has a great deal of wisdom, for it was just as he thought. Sammy was on hand bright and early every morning. He made sure that Old Man Coyote was nowhere in the Green Forest, and then he settled himself comfortably in the top of a tall pine tree where he could see all that was going on while Paddy the Beaver worked.

Paddy had finished his canal, and a beautiful canal it was, leading straight from his pond up to the aspen trees. As soon as he had finished it, he began to cut

[*177*]

the trees. As soon as one was down he would cut it into short lengths and roll them into the canal. Then he would float them out to his pond and over to his storehouse. He took the larger branches, on which there was sweet, tender bark, in the same way, for Paddy is never wasteful.

After a while he went over to his storehouse, which, you know, was nothing but a great pile of aspen logs and branches in his pond close by his house. He studied it very carefully. Then he swam back and climbed up on the bank of his canal.

"Mr. Jay," said he, "I think our work is about finished."

"What!" cried Sammy, "Aren't you going to cut the rest of those aspen trees?"

"No," replied Paddy. "Enough is always enough, and I've got enough to last me all winter. I want those trees for next year. Now I am fixed for the winter. I think I'll take it easy for a while."

Sammy looked disappointed. You see, he had just begun to learn that the greatest pleasure in the world comes from doing things for other people. For the first time since he could remember, someone wanted him around and it gave him such a good feeling down deep inside! Perhaps it was because he remembered that good feeling that the next spring he was so willing and anxious to help poor Mrs. Quack. What he did for her and all about her terrible adventures I will tell you in the next book.